The Little Prince

WRITTEN AND ILLUSTRATED BY
ANTOINE DE SAINT-EXUPÉRY

TRANSLATED FROM THE FRENCH BY
RICHARD HOWARD

THORNDIKE PRESS
A part of Gale, Cengage Learning

GALE
CENGAGE Learning

Detroit • New York • San Francisco • New Haven, Conn • Waterville, Maine • London

GALE
CENGAGE Learning

The little prince/by Antoine de Saint-Exupéry with drawings by the author; translated from the French by Richard Howard.

Published in 2005 by arrangement with Harcourt, Inc.

Thorndike Press® Large Print Classics.

The text of this Large Print edition is unabridged.
Other aspects of the book may vary from the original edition.

Set in 18 pt. Plantin by Minnie B. Raven.

Printed on permanent paper.

Library of Congress Cataloging-in-Publication Data
Saint-Exupéry, Antoine de, 1900–1944
    [Petit prince. English]
    The little prince / written and illustrated by Antoine
de Saint-Exupery ; translated from the French by
Richard Howard. — Large print ed.
        p. cm.
    Thorndike Press Large Print Classics.
    Summary: An aviator whose plane is forced down in the
Sahara Desert encounters a little prince from a small planet
who relates his adventures in seeking the secret of what is
important in life.
    ISBN 0-7862-7538-3 (lg. print : hc : alk. paper)
    ISBN 0-7862-7539-1 (lg. print : sc : alk. paper)
    1. Large type books. [1. Fairy tales. 2. Large type
books.] I. Howard, Richard, 1929– II. Title.
PZ8.S14Li 2005
[Fic]—dc22   2005000108

Printed in the United States of America
    2 3 4 5 6   19 18 17 16 15

TO LEON WERTH

I ask children to forgive me for dedicating this book to a grown-up. I have a serious excuse: this grown-up is the best friend I have in the world. I have another excuse: this grown-up can understand everything, even books for children. I have a third excuse: he lives in France where he is hungry and cold. He needs to be comforted. If all these excuses are not enough, then I want to dedicate this book to the child whom this grown-up once was. All grown-ups were children first. (But few of them remember it.) So I correct my dedication:

TO LEON WERTH
WHEN HE WAS A LITTLE BOY

In order to make his escape, I believe he took advantage of a migration of wild birds.

Translator's Note

In April 1943, *Le Petit Prince* was published in New York, a year before Antoine de Saint-Exupéry was shot down over the Mediterranean by German reconnaissance planes. The English translation, by Katherine Woods, was copyrighted the same year, and the work was dedicated in that translation to "the child who became Leon Werth. All grown-ups were once children — although few of them remember it."

As in the case of contemporaries like Mann and Gide (the latter a great admirer of Saint-Exupéry), new versions of "canonical" translations raise questions (or at least suspicions) of lèse-majesté. A second translator into

English of *The Little Prince* accepts the responsibility of such an imputation, for it must be acknowledged that all translations date; certain works never do. A new version of a work fifty-seven years old is entitled and, indeed, is obliged to persist further in the letter of that work. Each decade has its circumlocutions, its compliances; the translator seeks these out, as we see in Ms. Woods's pioneer endeavors, falls back on period makeshifts rather than confronting the often radical outrage of what the author, in his incomparable originality, ventures to say. The translator, it is seen in the fullness of time, so rarely *ventures* in this fashion, but rather falls back, as I say. It is the peculiar privilege of the *next* translator, in his own day and age, to sally forth, to be inordinate instead of placating or merely plausible. Time reveals all translation to be paraphrase, and it is in the longing for a *standard version* of a "beloved" work that we must begin again, we translators — that we must overtake one another.

R. H.
June 2000

I

Once when I was six I saw a magnificent picture in a book about the jungle, called *True Stories*. It showed a boa constrictor swallowing a wild beast. Here is a copy of the picture.

In the book it said: "Boa constrictors swallow their prey whole, without chewing. Afterward they are no longer able to move, and they sleep during the six months of their digestion."

In those days I thought a lot about jungle adventures, and eventually managed to make my first drawing, using a colored pencil. My drawing Number One looked like this:

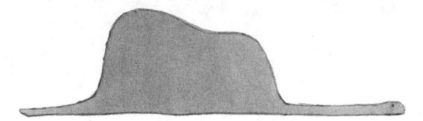

I showed the grown-ups my master-piece, and I asked them if my drawing scared them.

They answered, "Why be scared of a hat?"

My drawing was not a picture of a hat. It was a picture of a boa con-strictor digesting an elephant. Then I drew the inside of the boa constrictor, so the grown-ups could understand. They always need explanations. My drawing Number Two looked like this:

The grown-ups advised me to put away my drawings of boa constrictors, outside or inside, and apply myself instead to geography, history, arithmetic, and grammar. That is why I abandoned, at the age of six, a magnificent career as an artist. I had been discouraged by the failure of my drawing Number One and of my drawing Number Two. Grown-ups never understand anything by themselves, and it is exhausting for children to have to provide explanations over and over again.

So then I had to choose another career, and I learned to pilot airplanes. I have flown almost everywhere in the world. And, as a matter of fact, geography has been a big help to me. I could tell China from Arizona at first glance, which is very useful if you get lost during the night.

So I have had, in the course of my life, lots of encounters with lots of serious people. I have spent lots of time with grown-ups. I have seen them at close range . . . which hasn't much improved my opinion of them.

Whenever I encountered a grown-up who seemed to me at all enlightened, I would experiment on him with my drawing Number One, which I have always kept. I wanted to see if he really understood anything. But he would always answer, "That's a hat." Then I wouldn't talk about boa constrictors or jungles or stars. I would put myself on his level and talk about bridge and golf and politics and neckties. And my grown-up was glad to know such a reasonable person.

II

So I lived all alone, without anyone I could really talk to, until I had to make a crash landing in the Sahara Desert six years ago. Something in my plane's engine had broken, and since I had neither a mechanic nor passengers in the plane with me, I

was preparing to undertake the difficult repair job by myself. For me it
was a matter of life or death: I had
only enough drinking water for eight
days.

The first night, then, I went to sleep
on the sand a thousand miles from
any inhabited country. I was more
isolated than a man shipwrecked on a
raft in the middle of the ocean. So
you can imagine my surprise when I
was awakened at daybreak by a funny
little voice saying, "Please . . . draw
me a sheep . . ."

"What?"

"Draw me a sheep . . ."

I leaped up as if I had been struck
by lightning. I rubbed my eyes hard. I
stared. And I saw an extraordinary
little fellow staring back at me very
seriously. Here is the best portrait I

managed to make of him, later on. But of course my drawing is much less attractive than my model. This is not my fault. My career as a painter was discouraged at the age of six by the grown-ups, and I had never learned to draw anything except boa constrictors, outside and inside.

So I stared wide-eyed at this apparition. Don't forget that I was a thousand miles from any inhabited territory. Yet this little fellow seemed to be neither lost nor dying of exhaustion, hunger, or thirst; nor did he seem scared to death. There was nothing in his appearance that suggested a child lost in the middle of the desert a thousand miles from any inhabited territory. When I finally managed to speak, I asked him, "But . . . what are you doing here?"

And then he repeated, very slowly and very seriously, "Please . . . draw me a sheep . . ."

In the face of an overpowering mystery, you don't dare disobey. Absurd as it seemed, a thousand miles from all inhabited regions and in danger of death, I took a scrap of paper and a pen out of my pocket. But then I remembered that I had mostly studied geography, history, arithmetic, and grammar, and I told the little fellow (rather crossly) that I didn't know how to draw.

He replied, "That doesn't matter. Draw me a sheep."

Since I had never drawn a sheep, I made him one of the only two drawings I knew how to make — the one of the boa constrictor from outside. And I was astounded to hear the little fellow answer:

Here is the best portrait I managed to make of him, later on.

 "No! No! I don't want an elephant inside a boa constrictor. A boa constrictor is very dangerous, and an elephant would get in the way. Where I live, everything is very small. I need a sheep. Draw me a sheep."

So then I made a drawing.

He looked at it carefully, and then said, "No. This one is already quite sick. Make another."

I made an-other drawing. My friend gave me a kind, indulgent smile:

"You can see for yourself . . . that's not a sheep, it's a ram. It has horns . . ."

So I made my third drawing, but it was rejected, like the others:

"This one's too old. I want a sheep that will live a long time."

So then, impatiently, since I was in a hurry to start work on my engine, I scribbled this drawing, and added, "This is just the crate. The sheep you want is inside."

But I was amazed to see my young critic's face light up. "That's just the kind I wanted! Do you think this sheep will need a lot of grass?"

"Why?"

"Because where I live, everything is very small . . ."

"There's sure to be enough. I've given you a very small sheep."

He bent over the drawing. "Not so small as all that . . . Look! He's gone to sleep . . ."

And that's how I made the acquaintance of the little prince.

III

It took me a long time to understand where he came from. The little prince, who asked me so many questions, never seemed to hear the ones I asked him. It was things he said quite at random that, bit by bit, explained everything. For instance, when he first caught sight of my airplane (I won't draw my airplane; that would be much too complicated for me) he asked:

"What's that thing over there?"

"It's not a thing. It flies. It's an airplane. My airplane."

And I was proud to tell him I could fly. Then he exclaimed:

"What! You fell out of the sky?"

"Yes," I said modestly.

"Oh! That's funny . . ." And the little prince broke into a lovely peal of laughter, which annoyed me a good deal. I like my misfortunes to be taken seriously. Then he added, "So you fell out of the sky, too. What planet are you from?"

That was when I had the

first clue to the mystery of his presence, and I questioned him sharply. "Do you come from another planet?"

But he made no answer. He shook his head a little, still staring at my airplane. "Of course, *that* couldn't have brought you from very far . . ." And he fell into a reverie that lasted a long while. Then, taking my sheep out of his pocket, he plunged into contemplation of his treasure.

You can imagine how intrigued I was by this hint about "other planets." I tried to learn more: "Where do you come from, little fellow? Where is this 'where I live' of yours? Where will you be taking my sheep?"

After a thoughtful silence he answered, "The good thing about the crate you've given me is that he can use it for a house after dark."

"Of course. And if you're good, I'll give you a rope to tie him up during the day. And a stake to tie him to."

This proposition seemed to shock the little prince.

"Tie him up? What a funny idea!"

"But if you don't tie him up, he'll wander off somewhere and get lost."

My friend burst out laughing again. "Where could he go?"

"Anywhere. Straight ahead . . ."

Then the little prince remarked quite seriously, "Even if he did, everything's so small where I live!" And he added, perhaps a little sadly, "Straight ahead, you can't go very far."

IV

That was how I had learned a second very important thing, which was that the planet he came from was hardly bigger than a house!

That couldn't surprise me much. I knew very well that except for the huge planets like Earth, Jupiter, Mars, and Venus, which have been given names, there are hundreds of  others that are sometimes so small that it's very difficult to see them through a telescope. When an astronomer discovers one of them, he gives it a number instead of a name. For instance, he would call it "Asteroid 325."

I have serious reasons to believe that the planet the little prince came  from is Asteroid B-612. This asteroid has been sighted only once by telescope, in 1909 by a Turkish astronomer, who had then made a formal demonstration of his discovery at an International Astronomical Congress. But no one had believed him on account of the way he was dressed. Grown-ups are like that.

Fortunately for the reputation of

Asteroid B-612, a Turkish dictator ordered his people, on pain of death, to wear European clothes. The astronomer repeated his demonstration in 1920, wearing a very elegant suit. And this time everyone believed him.

If I've told you these details about Asteroid B-612 and if I've given you its number, it is on account of the grown-ups. Grown-ups like numbers. When you tell them about a new friend, they  never ask questions about what really matters. They never ask: "What does his voice sound like?" "What games does he like best?" "Does he collect

28

The Little Prince on Asteroid B-612

butterflies?" They ask: "How old is he?" "How many brothers does he have?" "How much does he weigh?" "How much money does his father make?" Only then do they think they know him. If you tell grown-ups, "I saw a beautiful red brick house, with geraniums at the windows and doves on the roof . . . ," they won't be able to imagine such a house. You have to tell them, "I saw a house worth a hundred thousand francs." Then they exclaim, "What a pretty house!"

So if you tell them: "The proof of the little prince's existence is that he was delightful, that he laughed, and that he wanted a sheep. When someone wants a sheep, that proves he exists," they shrug their shoulders and treat you like a child! But if you tell them, "The planet he came from is Asteroid B-612," then they'll be convinced, and they won't bother you with their questions. That's the way they are. You must not hold it against them. Children should be very understanding of grown-ups.

But, of course, those of us who understand life couldn't care less about numbers! I should have liked to begin this story like a fairy tale. I should have liked to say:

"Once upon a time there was a little prince who lived on a planet hardly any bigger than he was, and who needed a friend . . ." For those who understand life, that would sound much truer.

The fact is, I don't want my book to be taken lightly. Telling these memories is so painful for me. It's already been six years since my friend went away, taking his sheep with him. If I try to describe him here, it's so I won't forget him. It's sad to forget a friend. Not everyone has had a friend. And I might become like the grown-ups who are no longer interested in anything but numbers. Which is still another reason why I've bought a box of paints and some pencils. It's hard to go back to drawing, at my age, when you've never made any attempts since the one of a boa from inside and the one of a boa from outside, at the age of six! I'll certainly try to make my portraits as true to life as possible. But I'm not entirely sure of succeeding. One drawing works, and the next no longer bears any resemblance. And I'm a little off on his height, too. In this one the little prince is too tall. And here he's too short. And I'm uncertain about the color of his suit. So I grope in one direction and another, as best I can. In the end, I'm sure to get certain more important details all wrong. But here you'll have to forgive me. My friend never explained anything. Perhaps he thought I was like himself. But I, unfortunately, cannot see a sheep through the sides of a crate. I may be a little like the grown-ups. I must have grown old.

V

Every day I'd learn something about the little prince's planet, about his departure, about his journey. It would come quite gradually, in the course of his remarks. This was how I learned, on the third day, about the drama of the baobabs.

This time, too, I had the sheep to thank, for suddenly the little prince asked me a question, as if overcome by a grave doubt.

"Isn't it true that sheep eat bushes?"

"Yes, that's right."

"Ah! I'm glad."

I didn't understand why it was so important that sheep should eat bushes. But the little prince added:

"And therefore they eat baobabs, too?"

I pointed out to the little prince that baobabs are not bushes but trees as tall as churches, and that even if he took a whole herd of elephants back to his planet, that herd couldn't finish off a single baobab.

The idea of the herd of elephants made the little prince laugh.

"We'd have to pile them on top of one another."

But he observed perceptively:

"Before they grow big, baobabs start out by being little."

"True enough! But why do you want your sheep to eat little baobabs?"

He answered, "Oh, come on! You know!" as if we were talking about something quite obvious. And I was forced to make a great mental effort to understand this problem all by myself.

And, in fact, on

the little prince's planet there were —
as on all planets — good plants and
bad plants. The good plants come
from good seeds, and the bad plants
from bad seeds. But the seeds are invisible. They sleep in the secrecy of
the ground until one of them decides
to wake up. Then it stretches and be-
gins to sprout, quite timidly at first, a
charming, harmless little twig
reaching toward the sun. If it's a
radish seed, or a rosebush seed, you
can let it sprout all it likes. But if it's
the seed of a bad plant, you must pull
the plant up right away, as soon as
you can recognize it. As it happens,
there were terrible seeds on the little
prince's planet . . . baobab seeds. The
planet's soil was infested with them.
Now if you attend to a baobab too
late, you can never get rid of it again.

It overgrows the whole planet. Its roots pierce right through. And if the planet is too small, and if there are too many baobabs, they make it burst into pieces.

"It's a question of discipline," the little prince told me later on. "When you've finished washing and dressing each morning, you must tend your planet. You must be sure you pull up the baobabs regularly, as soon as you can tell them apart from the rose-bushes, which they closely resemble when they're very young. It's very tedious work, but very easy."

And one day he advised me to do my best to make a beautiful drawing, for the edification of the children where I live. "If they travel someday," he told me, "it could be useful to them. Sometimes there's no harm in postponing your work until later. But with baobabs, it's always a catastrophe. I knew one planet that was inhabited by a lazy man. He had neglected three bushes . . ."

So, following the little prince's instructions, I have drawn that planet. I don't much like assuming the tone of a moralist. But the danger of baobabs is so little recognized, and the risks run by anyone who might get lost on an asteroid are so considerable, that for once I am making an exception to my habitual reserve. I say, "Children, watch out for baobabs!" It's to warn my friends of a danger of which they, like myself, have long been unaware that I worked so hard on this drawing. The lesson I'm teaching is worth the trouble. You may be asking, "Why are there no other drawings in this book as big as the drawing of the baobabs?" There's a simple answer: I tried but I couldn't manage it. When I drew the baobabs, I was inspired by a sense of urgency.

VI

O little prince! Gradually, this was how I came to understand your sad

The Baobabs

40

little life. For a long time your only entertainment was the pleasure of sunsets. I learned this new detail on the morning of the fourth day, when you told me:

"I really like sunsets. Let's go look at one now . . ."

"But we have to wait . . ."

"What for?"

"For the sun to set."

At first you seemed quite surprised, and then you laughed at your-you said to me, "I think I'm still at home!"

Indeed. When it's noon in the United States, the sun, as everyone knows, is setting over France. If you could fly to France in one minute, you could watch the sunset. Unfortunately France is much too far. But on your tiny planet, all you had to do was move your chair a few feet. And you would watch the twilight whenever you wanted to. . . .

"One day I saw the sun set forty-four times!" And a little later you added, "You know, when you're feeling very sad, sunsets are wonderful . . ."

"On the day of the forty-four times, were you feeling very sad?"

But the little prince didn't answer.

VII

On the fifth day, thanks again to the sheep, another secret of the little prince's life was revealed to me. Abruptly, with no preamble, he asked me, as if it were the fruit of a problem long pondered in silence:

"If a sheep eats bushes, does it eat flowers, too?"

"A sheep eats whatever it finds."

"Even flowers that have thorns?"

"Yes. Even flowers that have thorns."

"Then what good are thorns?"

I didn't know. At that moment I was very busy trying to unscrew a bolt that had got jammed in my engine. I was quite worried, for my plane crash was beginning to seem extremely serious, and the lack of drinking water made me fear the worst.

"What good are thorns?"

The little prince never let go of a question once he had asked it. I was annoyed by my jammed bolt, and I answered without thinking.

"Thorns are no good for anything — they're just the flowers' way of being mean!"

"Oh!" But after a silence, he lashed out at me, with a sort of bitterness. "I don't believe you! Flowers are weak. They're naive. They reassure themselves whatever way they can. They believe their thorns make them frightening . . ."

I made no answer. At that moment I was thinking, *If this bolt stays jammed, I'll knock it off with the hammer.* Again the little prince disturbed my reflections.

"Then you think flowers . . ."

"No, not at all. I don't think any-thing! I just said whatever came into my head. I'm busy here with some-thing serious!"

He stared at me, astounded.

" 'Something serious'!"

He saw me holding my hammer, my fingers black with grease, bending over an object he regarded as very ugly.

"You talk like the grown-ups!"

That made me a little ashamed. But he added, mercilessly:

"You confuse everything . . . You've got it all mixed up!" He was really very annoyed. He tossed his golden curls in the wind. "I know a planet inhabited by a red-faced gen-tleman. He's never smelled a flower. He's never looked at a star. He's never loved anyone. He's never done anything except add up numbers. And all day long he says over and over, just like you, 'I'm a serious man! I'm a serious man!' And that puffs him up with pride. But he's not a man at all — he's a mushroom!"

"He's a what?"

"A mushroom!" The little prince was now quite pale with rage. "For millions of years flowers have been producing thorns. For millions of years sheep have been eating them all the same. And it's not serious, trying to understand why flowers go to such trouble to produce thorns that are good for nothing? It's not important, the war between the sheep and the flowers? It's no more serious and more important than the numbers that fat red gentleman is adding up?

Suppose I happen to know a unique flower, one that exists nowhere in the world except on my planet, one that a little sheep can wipe out in a single bite one morning, just like that, without even realizing what he's doing — that isn't important?" His face turned red now, and he went on. "If someone loves a flower of which just one example exists among all the millions and millions of stars, that's enough to make him happy when he looks at the stars. He tells himself, 'My flower's up there somewhere . . .' But if the sheep eats the flower, then for him it's as if, suddenly, all the stars went out. And that isn't important?"

He couldn't say another word. All of a sudden he burst out sobbing. Night had fallen. I dropped my tools. What did I care about my hammer,

about my bolt, about
thirst and death? There
was, on one star, on
one planet, on mine,
the Earth, a little prince
to be consoled! I took
him in my arms. I rocked him. I told
him, "The flower you love is not in
danger . . . I'll draw you a muzzle for
your sheep . . . I'll draw you a fence
for your flower . . . I . . ." I didn't
know what to say. How clumsy I felt!
I didn't know how to reach him,
where to find him. . . . It's so mysterious, the land of tears.

VIII

I soon learned to know that flower
better. On the little prince's planet,

there had always been very simple flowers, decorated with a single row of petals so that they took up no room at all and got in no one's way. They would appear one morning in the grass, and would fade by nightfall. But this one had grown from a seed brought from who knows where, and the little prince had kept a close watch over a sprout that was not like any of the others. It might have been a new kind of baobab. But the

sprout soon stopped growing and began to show signs of blossoming. The little prince, who had watched the development of an enormous bud, realized that some sort of miraculous apparition would emerge from it, but the flower continued her beauty preparations in the shelter of her green chamber, selecting her colors with the greatest care and dressing quite deliberately, adjusting her petals one by one. She had no desire to emerge all rumpled, like the poppies. She wished to appear only in the full radiance of her beauty. Oh yes, she was quite vain! And her mysterious adornment had lasted days and days. And then one morning, precisely at sunrise, she showed herself.

And after having labored so pains-

takingly, she yawned and said, "Ah!
I'm hardly awake . . . Forgive me . . .
I'm still all untidy . . ."

But the little prince couldn't con-
tain his admiration.

"How lovely you are!"

"Aren't I?" the flower answered
sweetly. "And I was born the same
time as the sun . . ."

The little prince realized that she
wasn't any too modest, but she was so
dazzling!

"I believe it is breakfast time," she

had soon added. "Would you be so kind as to tend to me?"

And the little prince, utterly abashed, having gone to look for a watering can, served the flower.

She had soon begun tormenting him with her rather touchy vanity. One day, for instance, alluding to her four thorns, she remarked to the little prince, "I'm ready for tigers, with all their claws!"

"There are no tigers on my planet," the little prince had objected, "and

besides, tigers don't eat weeds."

"I am not a weed," the flower sweetly replied.

"Forgive me . . ."

"I am not at all afraid of tigers, but I have a horror of drafts. You wouldn't happen to have a screen?"

"A horror of drafts . . . that's not a good sign, for a plant," the little prince had observed. "How complicated this flower is . . ."

"After dark you will put me under glass. How cold it is where you live —

quite uncomfortable. Where I come from —" But she suddenly broke off. She had come here as a seed. She couldn't have known anything of other worlds. Humiliated at having let herself be caught on the verge of so naive a lie, she coughed two or three times in order to put the little prince in the wrong. "That screen?"

"I was going to look for one, but you were speaking to me!"

Then she made herself cough again, in order to inflict a twinge of remorse on him all the same.

So the little prince, despite all the goodwill of his love, had soon come to mistrust her. He had taken seriously certain inconsequential remarks and had grown very unhappy.

"I shouldn't have listened to her,"

he confided to me one day. "You must never listen to flowers. You must look at them and smell them. Mine perfumed my planet, but I didn't know how to enjoy that. The business about the tiger claws, instead of annoying me, ought to have moved me . . ."

And he confided further, "In those days, I didn't understand anything. I should have judged her according to her actions, not her words. She perfumed my planet and lit up my life. I should never have run away! I ought to have realized the tenderness underlying her silly pretensions. Flowers are so contradictory! But I was too young to know how to love her."

IX

In order to make his escape, I believe he took advantage of a migration of wild birds. On the morning of his departure, he put his planet in order. He carefully raked out his active volcanoes. The little prince possessed two active volcanoes, which were very convenient for warming his breakfast. He also possessed one extinct volcano. But, as he said, "You never know!" So he raked out the extinct volcano, too. If they are properly raked out, volcanoes burn gently and regularly, without eruptions. Volcanic eruptions are like fires in a chimney. Of course, on our Earth we are much too small to rake out our volcanoes. That is why they cause us so much trouble.

The little prince also uprooted, a little sadly, the last baobab shoots. He believed he would never be coming back. But all these familiar tasks seemed very sweet to him on this last morning. And when he watered the flower one last time, and put her under glass, he felt like crying.

"Good-bye," he said to the flower.

But she did not answer him.

"Good-bye," he repeated.

The flower coughed. But not because she had a cold.

"I've been silly," she told him at last. "I ask your forgiveness. Try to be happy."

He was surprised that there were no reproaches. He stood there, quite bewildered, holding the glass bell in midair. He failed to understand this calm sweetness.

"Of course I love you," the flower told him. "It was my fault you never knew. It doesn't matter. But you were just as silly as I was. Try to be happy . . . Put that glass thing down. I don't want it anymore."

"But the wind . . ."

"My cold isn't that bad . . . The night air will do me good. I'm a flower."

"But the animals . . ."

He carefully raked out his active volcanoes.

"I need to put up with two or three caterpillars if I want to get to know the butterflies. Apparently they're very beautiful. Otherwise who will visit me? You'll be far away. As for the big animals, I'm not afraid of them. I have my own claws." And she naively showed her four thorns. Then she added, "Don't hang around like this; it's irritating. You made up your mind to leave. Now go."

For she didn't want him to see her crying. She was such a proud flower. . . .

X

He happened to be in the vicinity of Asteroids 325, 326, 327, 328, 329, and 330. So he began by visiting them, to keep himself busy and to learn something.

The first one was inhabited by a king. Wearing purple and ermine, he was sitting on a simple yet majestic throne.

"Ah! Here's a subject!" the king exclaimed when he caught sight of the little prince.

And the little prince wondered,

How can he know who I am if he's never seen me before? He didn't realize that for kings, the world is extremely simplified: All men are subjects.

"Approach the throne so I can get a better look at you," said the king, very proud of being a king for someone at last.

The little prince looked around for a place to sit down, but the planet was covered by the magnificent ermine cloak. So he remained standing, and since he was tired, he yawned.

"It is a violation of etiquette to yawn in a king's presence," the monarch told him. "I forbid you to do so."

"I can't help it," answered the little prince, quite embarrassed. "I've made a long journey, and I haven't had any sleep . . ."

"Then I command you to yawn,"

said the king. "I haven't seen anyone yawn for years. For me, yawns are a curiosity. Come on, yawn again! It is an order."

"That intimidates me . . . I can't do it now," said the little prince, blushing deeply.

"Well, well!" the king replied. "Then I . . . I command you to yawn sometimes and sometimes to . . ."

He was sputtering a little, and seemed annoyed.

For the king insisted that his authority be universally respected. He would tolerate no disobedience, being an absolute monarch. But since he was a kindly man, all his commands were reasonable. "If I were to command," he would often say, "if I were to command a general to turn into a seagull, and if the general did not obey, that would not be the general's fault. It would be mine."

"May I sit down?" the little prince timidly inquired.

"I command you to sit down," the king replied, majestically gathering up a fold of his ermine robe.

But the little prince was wondering. The planet was tiny. Over what could the king really reign? "Sire . . . ," he ventured, "excuse me for asking . . ."

"I command you to ask," the king hastened to say.

"Sire . . . over what do you reign?"

"Over everything," the king answered, with great simplicity.

"Over everything?"

With a discreet gesture the king pointed to his planet, to the other planets, and to the stars.

"Over all that?" asked the little prince.

"Over all that . . . ," the king answered.

For not only was he an absolute monarch, but a universal monarch as well.

"And do the stars obey you?"

"Of course," the king replied. "They obey immediately. I tolerate no insubordination."

Such power amazed the little prince. If he had wielded it himself, he could have watched not forty-four but seventy-two, or even a hundred, even two hundred sunsets on the same day without ever having to move his chair! And since he was feeling rather sad on account of remembering his own little planet, which he had forsaken, he ventured to ask a favor of the king: "I'd like to see a sunset . . . Do me a favor, your majesty . . . Command the sun to set . . ."

"If I commanded a general to fly from one flower to the next like a butterfly, or to write a tragedy, or to turn into a seagull, and if the general did not carry out my command, which of us would be in the wrong, the general or me?"

"You would be," said the little prince, quite firmly.

"Exactly. One must command from each what each can perform," the king went on. "Authority is based first of all upon reason. If you command your subjects to jump in the ocean, there will be a revolution. I am entitled to command obedience because my orders are reasonable."

"Then my sunset?" insisted the little prince, who never let go of a question once he had asked it.

"You shall have your sunset. I shall command it. But I shall wait, according to my science of government, until conditions are favorable."

"And when will that be?" inquired the little prince.

"Well, well!" replied the king, first consulting a large calendar. "Well, well! That will be around . . . around . . . that will be tonight around seven-forty! And you'll see how well I am obeyed."

The little prince yawned. He was regretting his lost sunset. And besides, he was already growing a little bored. "I have nothing further to do here," he told the king. "I'm going to be on my way!"

"Do not leave!" answered the king, who was so proud of having a subject. "Do not leave; I shall make you my minister!"

"A minister of what?"

"Of . . . of justice!"

"But there's no one here to judge!"

"You never know," the king told him. "I have not yet explored the whole of my realm. I am very old, I have no room for a carriage, and it wearies me to walk."

"Oh, but I've already seen for myself," said the little prince, leaning forward to glance one more time at the other side of the planet. "There's no one over there, either . . ."

"Then you shall pass judgment on yourself," the king answered. "That is the hardest thing of all. It is much harder to judge yourself than to judge others. If you succeed in judging yourself, it's because you are truly a wise man."

"But I can judge myself anywhere," said the little prince. "I don't need to live here."

"Well, well!" the king said. "I have good reason to believe that there is an old rat living somewhere on my planet. I hear him at night. You could judge that old rat. From time to time you will condemn him to death. That way his life will depend on your justice. But you'll pardon him each time for economy's sake. There's only one rat."

"I don't like condemning anyone to death," the little prince said, "and now I think I'll be on my way."

"No," said the king.

The little prince, having completed

his preparations, had no desire to aggrieve the old monarch. "If Your Majesty desires to be promptly obeyed, he should give me a reasonable command. He might command me, for instance, to leave before this minute is up. It seems to me that conditions are favorable . . ."

The king having made no answer, the little prince hesitated at first, and then, with a sigh, took his leave.

"I make you my ambassador," the king hastily shouted after him. He had a great air of authority.

"Grown-ups are so strange," the little prince said to himself as he went on his way.

XI

The second planet was inhabited by a very vain man.

"Ah! A visit from an admirer!" he exclaimed when he caught sight of the little prince, still at some distance. To vain men, other people are admirers.

"Hello," said the little prince. "That's a funny hat you're wearing."

"It's for answering acclamations," the very vain man replied. "Unfortunately, no one ever comes this way."

"Is that so?" said the little prince, who did not understand what the vain man was talking about.

"Clap your hands," directed the man.

The little prince clapped his hands,

and the very vain man tipped his hat in modest acknowledgment.

This is more entertaining than the visit to the king, the little prince said to himself. And he continued clapping. The very vain man continued tipping his hat in acknowledgment.

After five minutes of this exercise, the little prince tired of the game's monotony. "And what would make the hat fall off?" he asked.

But the vain man did not hear him. Vain men never hear anything but praise.

"Do you really admire me a great

deal?" he asked the little prince.

"What does that mean — *admire?*"

"*To admire* means to acknowledge that I am the handsomest, the best-dressed, the richest, and the most intelligent man on the planet."

"But you're the only man on your planet!"

"Do me this favor. Admire me all the same."

"I admire you," said the little prince, with a little shrug of his shoulders, "but what is there about my admiration that interests you so much?" And the little prince went on his way.

"Grown-ups are certainly very strange," he said to himself as he continued on his journey.

XII

The next planet was inhabited by a drunkard. This visit was a very brief one, but it plunged the little prince into a deep depression.

"What are you doing there?" he asked the drunkard, whom he found sunk in silence before a collection of empty bottles and a collection of full ones.

"Drinking," replied the drunkard, with a gloomy expression.

"Why are you drinking?" the little prince asked.

"To forget," replied the drunkard.

"To forget what?" inquired the little prince, who was already feeling sorry for him.

"To forget that I'm ashamed,"

confessed the drunkard, hanging his head.

"What are you ashamed of?" inquired the little prince, who wanted to help.

"Of drinking!" concluded the drunkard, withdrawing into silence for good. And the little prince went

on his way, puzzled.

"Grown-ups are certainly very, very strange," he said to himself as he continued on his journey.

XIII

The fourth planet belonged to a businessman. This person was so busy that he didn't even raise his head when the little prince arrived.

"Hello," said the little prince. "Your cigarette's gone out."

"Three and two make five. Five and seven, twelve. Twelve and three, fifteen. Hello. Fifteen and seven, twenty-two. Twenty-two and six, twenty-eight. No time to light it again. Twenty-six and five, thirty-one. Whew! That amounts to five-hundred-and-one million, six-hundred-twenty-two thousand, seven hundred thirty-one."

"Five-hundred million what?"

"Hmm? You're still there? Five-hundred-and-one million . . . I don't remember . . . I have so much work to do! I'm a serious man. I can't be bothered with trifles! Two and five,

seven . . ."

"Five-hundred-and-one million what?" repeated the little prince, who had never in his life let go of a question once he had asked it.

The businessman raised his head. "For the fifty-four years I've inhabited this planet, I've been interrupted only three times. The first time was twenty-two years ago, when I was interrupted by a beetle that had fallen onto my desk from god knows where. It made a terrible noise, and I made four mistakes in my calculations. The second time was eleven years ago, when I was interrupted by a fit of rheumatism. I don't get enough exercise. I haven't time to take strolls. I'm a serious person. The third time . . . is right now! Where was I? Five-hundred-and-one million . . ."

"Million what?"

The businessman realized that he had no hope of being left in peace. "Oh, of those little things you sometimes see in the sky."

"Flies?"

"No, those little shiny things."

"Bees?"

"No, those little golden things that make lazy people daydream. Now, I'm a serious person. I have no time for daydreaming."

"Ah! You mean the stars?"

"Yes, that's it. Stars."

"And what do you do with five-hundred million stars?"

"Five-hundred-and-one million, six-hundred-twenty-two thousand, seven hundred thirty-one. I'm a serious person, and I'm accurate."

"And what do you do with those stars?"

"What do I do with them?"

"Yes."

"Nothing. I own them."

"You own the stars?"

79

"Yes."

"But I've already seen a king who —"

"Kings don't own. They 'reign' over . . . It's quite different."

"And what good does owning the stars do you?"

"It does me the good of being rich."

"And what good does it do you to be rich?"

"It lets me buy other stars, if somebody discovers them."

The little prince said to himself, *This man argues a little like my drunkard.* Nevertheless he asked more questions. "How can someone own the stars?"

"To whom do they belong?" retorted the businessman grumpily.

"I don't know. To nobody."

"Then they belong to me, because I

thought of it first."

"And that's all it takes?"

"Of course. When you find a diamond that belongs to nobody in particular, then it's yours. When you find an island that belongs to nobody in particular, it's yours. When you're the first person to have an idea, you patent it and it's yours. Now I own the stars, since no one before me ever thought of owning them."

"That's true enough," the little prince said. "And what do you do with them?"

"I manage them. I count them and then count them again," the businessman said. "It's difficult work. But I'm a serious person!"

The little prince was still not satisfied. "If I own a scarf, I can tie it around my neck and take it away. If I own a flower, I can pick it and take it away. But you can't pick the stars!"

"No, but I can put them in the bank."

"What does that mean?"

"That means that I write the number of my stars on a slip of paper. And then I lock that slip of paper in a drawer."

"And that's all?"

"That's enough!"

That's amusing, thought the little prince. *And even poetic. But not very serious.* The little prince had very different ideas about serious things from those of the grown-ups. "I own a flower myself," he continued, "which I water every day. I own three volcanoes, which I rake out every week. I even rake out the extinct one. You never know. It's of some use to my volcanoes, and it's useful to my flower, that I own them. But you're not useful to the stars."

The businessman opened his mouth but found nothing to say in reply, and the little prince went on his way.

"Grown-ups are certainly quite extraordinary" was all he said to himself as he continued on his journey.

XIV

The fifth planet was very strange. It was the smallest of all. There was just enough room for a street lamp and a lamplighter. The little prince couldn't quite understand what use a street lamp and a lamplighter could be up there in the sky, on a planet without any people and not a single house. However, he said to himself, *It's quite possible that this man is absurd. But he's less absurd than the king, the very vain man, the businessman, and the drunkard. At least his work has some meaning. When he lights his lamp, it's as if he's bringing one more star to life, or one more flower. When he puts out his lamp, that sends the flower or the star to sleep. Which is a fine occupation. And therefore truly useful.*

When the little prince reached this planet, he greeted the lamplighter respectfully. "Good morning. Why have you just put out your lamp?"

"Orders," the lamplighter answered. "Good morning."

"What orders are those?"

"To put out my street lamp. Good evening." And he lit his lamp again.

"But why have you just lit your

"It's a terrible job I have."

lamp again?"

"Orders."

"I don't understand," said the little prince.

"There's nothing to understand," said the lamplighter. "Orders are orders. Good morning." And he put out his lamp. Then he wiped his forehead with a red-checked handkerchief. "It's a terrible job I have. It used to be reasonable enough. I put the lamp out mornings and lit it after dark. I had the rest of the day for my own affairs, and the rest of the night for sleeping."

"And since then orders have changed?"

"Orders haven't changed," the lamplighter said. "That's just the trouble! Year by year the planet is turning faster and faster, and orders haven't changed!"

"Which means?"

"Which means that now that the planet revolves once a minute, I don't have an instant's rest. I light my lamp and turn it out once every minute!"

"That's funny! Your days here are one minute long!"

"It's not funny at all," the lamplighter said. "You and I have already been talking to each other for a month."

"A month?"

"Yes. Thirty minutes. Thirty days! Good evening." And he lit his lamp.

The little prince watched him, growing fonder and fonder of this lamplighter who was so faithful to orders. He remembered certain sunsets that he himself used to follow in other days, merely by shifting his chair. He wanted to help his friend.

"You know . . . I can show you a way to take a rest whenever you want to."

"I always want to rest," the lamplighter said, for it is possible to be faithful and lazy at the same time.

The little prince continued, "Your planet is so small that you can walk around it in three strides. All you have to do is walk more slowly, and you'll always be in the sun. When you want to take a rest just walk . . . and the day will last as long as you want it to."

"What good does that do me," the lamplighter said, "when the one thing in life I want to do is sleep?"

"Then you're out of luck," said the little prince.

"I am," said the lamplighter. "Good

morning." And he put out his lamp.

Now that man, the little prince said to himself as he continued on his journey, *that man would be despised by all the others, by the king, by the very vain man, by the drunkard, by the businessman. Yet he's the only one who doesn't strike me as ridiculous. Perhaps it's because he's thinking of something besides himself.* He heaved a sigh of regret and said to himself, again, *That man is the only one I might have made my friend. But his planet is really too small. There's not room for two . . .*

What the little prince dared not admit was that he most regretted leaving that planet because it was blessed with one thousand, four hundred forty sunsets every twenty-four hours!

XV

The sixth planet was ten times bigger than the last. It was inhabited by an old gentleman who wrote enormous books.

"Ah, here comes an explorer," he exclaimed when he caught sight of the little prince, who was feeling a little winded and sat down on the desk. He had already traveled so much and so far!

"Where do you come from?" the old gentleman asked him.

"What's that big book?" asked the little prince. "What do you do with it?"

"I'm a geographer," the old gentleman answered.

"And what's a geographer?"

"A scholar who knows where the seas are, and the rivers, the cities, the mountains, and the deserts."

"That is very interesting," the little prince said. "Here at last is someone who has a real profession!" And he gazed around him at the geographer's planet. He had never seen a planet so majestic. "Your planet is very beautiful," he said. "Does it have any oceans?"

"I couldn't say," said the geographer.

"Oh!" The little prince was disappointed. "And mountains?"

"I couldn't say," said the geographer.

"And cities and rivers and deserts?"

"I couldn't tell you that, either," the geographer said.

"But you're a geographer!"

"That's right," said the geographer, "but I'm not an explorer. There's not one explorer on my planet. A geographer doesn't go out to describe cities, rivers, mountains, seas, oceans, and deserts. A geographer is too important to go wandering about. He never leaves his study. But he receives the explorers there. He questions them, and he writes down what they remember. And if the memories of one of the explorers seem interesting to him, then the geographer conducts an inquiry into that explorer's moral character."

"Why is that?"

"Because an explorer who told lies would cause disasters in the geography books. As would an explorer who drank too much."

"Why is that?" the little prince asked again.

"Because drunkards see double. And the geographer would write down two mountains where there was only one."

"I know someone," said the little prince, "who would be a bad explorer."

"Possibly. Well, when the explorer's moral character seems to be a good one, an investigation is made into his discovery."

"By going to see it?"

"No, that would be too complicated. But the explorer is required to
furnish proofs. For instance, if he
claims to have discovered a large
mountain, he is required to bring
back large stones from it." The geographer suddenly grew excited. "But
you come from far away! You're an
explorer! You must describe your
planet for me!"

And the geographer, having opened
his logbook, sharpened his pencil.
Explorers' reports are first recorded
in pencil; ink is used only after proofs
have been furnished.

"Well?" said the geographer expec-
tantly.

"Oh, where I live," said the little
prince, "is not very interesting. It's so

small. I have three volcanoes, two active and one extinct. But you never know."

"You never know," said the geographer.

"I also have a flower."

"We don't record flowers," the geographer said.

"Why not? It's the prettiest thing!"

"Because flowers are ephemeral."

"What does *ephemeral* mean?"

"Geographies," said the geographer, "are the finest books of all. They never go out of fashion. It is extremely rare for a mountain to change position. It is extremely rare for an ocean to be drained of its water. We write eternal things."

"But extinct volcanoes can come back to life," the little prince interrupted. "What does *ephemeral* mean?"

"Whether volcanoes are extinct or active comes down to the same thing for us," said the geographer. "For us what counts is the mountain. That doesn't change."

"But what does *ephemeral* mean?" repeated the little prince, who had never in all his life let go of a question once he had asked it.

"It means, 'which is threatened by imminent disappearance.' "

"Is my flower threatened by imminent disappearance?"

"Of course."

My flower is ephemeral, the little prince said to himself, *and she has only four thorns with which to defend herself against the world! And I've left her all alone where I live!*

That was his first impulse of regret. But he plucked up his courage again.

"Where would you advise me to visit?" he asked.

"The planet Earth," the geographer answered. "It has a good reputation."

And the little prince went on his way, thinking about his flower.

XVI

The seventh planet, then, was the Earth.

The Earth is not just another planet! It contains one hundred and eleven kings (including, of course, the African kings), seven thousand geographers, nine-hundred thousand businessmen, seven-and-a-half million drunkards, three-hundred-eleven million egotists; in other words, about two billion grown-ups.

To give you a notion of the Earth's dimensions, I can tell you that before the invention of electricity, it was necessary to maintain, over the whole of six continents, a veritable army of four-hundred-sixty-two thousand, five hundred and eleven lamp-lighters.

Seen from some distance, this made a splendid effect. The move-ments of this army were ordered like those of a ballet. First came the turn of the lamplighters of New Zealand and Australia; then these, having lit their street lamps, would go home to sleep. Next it would be the turn of the lamplighters of China and Siberia to perform their steps in the lamplight-ers' ballet, and then they too would vanish into the wings. Then came the turn of the lamplighters of Russia and

India. Then those of Africa and Europe. Then those of South America, and of North America. And they never missed their cues for their appearances onstage. It was awe-inspiring.

Only the lamplighter of the single street lamp at the North Pole and his colleague of the single street lamp at the South Pole led carefree, idle lives: They worked twice a year.

XVII

Trying to be witty leads to lying, more or less. What I just told you about the lamplighters isn't completely true, and I risk giving a false idea of our planet to those who don't know it. Men occupy very little space on Earth. If the two billion inhabitants of the globe were to stand close together, as they might for some big public event, they would easily fit into a city block that was twenty miles long and twenty miles wide. You could crowd all humanity onto the smallest Pacific islet.

Grown-ups, of course, won't believe you. They're convinced they take up much more room. They consider themselves as important as the baobabs. So you should advise them to make their own calculations — they love numbers, and they'll enjoy it. But don't waste your time on this extra task. It's unnecessary. Trust me.

So once he reached Earth, the little prince was quite surprised not to see anyone. He was beginning to fear he had come to the wrong planet, when a moon-colored loop uncoiled on the sand.

"Good evening," the little prince said, just in case.

"Good evening," said the snake.

"What planet have I landed on?" asked the little prince.

"On the planet Earth, in Africa," the snake replied.

"Ah! . . . And are there no people on Earth?"

"It's the desert here. There are no people in the desert. Earth is very big," said the snake.

The little prince sat down on a rock and looked up into the sky.

"I wonder," he said, "if the stars are lit up so that each of us can find his own, someday. Look at my planet — it's just overhead. But so far away!"

"It's lovely," the snake said. "What

have you come to Earth for?"

"I'm having difficulties with a flower," the little prince said.

"Ah!" said the snake.

And they were both silent.

"Where are the people?" The little prince finally resumed the conversation. "It's a little lonely in the desert . . ."

"It's also lonely with people," said the snake.

The little prince looked at the snake for a long time. "You're a funny creature," he said at last, "no thicker than a finger."

"But I'm more powerful than a king's finger," the snake said.

The little prince smiled.

"You're not very powerful . . . You don't even have feet. You couldn't travel very far."

The little prince was quite surprised not
to see anyone.

103

"I can take you further than a ship," the snake said. He coiled around the little prince's ankle, like a golden bracelet. "Anyone I touch, I send back to the land from which he came," the snake went on. "But you're innocent, and you come from a star . . ."

The little prince made no reply.

"I feel sorry for you, being so weak on this granite earth," said the snake. "I can help you, someday, if you grow too homesick for your planet. I can —"

"Oh, I understand just what you mean," said the little prince, "but why do you always speak in riddles?"

"I solve them all," said the snake.

And they were both silent.

XVIII

The little prince crossed the desert and encountered only one flower. A flower with three petals — a flower of no consequence . . .

"Good morning," said the little prince.

"Good morning," said the flower.

"Where are the people?" the little prince inquired politely.

The flower had one day seen a caravan passing.

"People? There are six or seven of them, I believe, in existence. I caught sight of them years ago. But you never know where to find them. The wind blows them away. They have no roots, which hampers them a good deal."

"You're a funny creature, no thicker than a finger."

"Good-bye," said the little prince.
"Good-bye," said the flower.

XIX

The little prince climbed a high mountain. The only mountains he had ever known were the three volcanoes, which came up to his knee. And he used the extinct volcano as a footstool. *From a mountain as high as this one,* he said to himself, *I'll get a view of the whole planet and all the people on it* . . . But he saw nothing but rocky peaks as sharp as needles.

"Hello," he said, just in case.

"Hello . . . hello . . . hello . . . ," the echo answered.

"Who are you?" asked the little prince.

"Who are you . . . who are you . . . who are you . . . ," the echo answered.

"Let's be friends. I'm lonely," he said.

"I'm lonely . . . I'm lonely . . . I'm lonely . . . ," the echo answered.

What a peculiar planet! he thought. *It's all dry and sharp and hard. And people here have no imagination. They repeat whatever you say to them. Where I live I had a flower: She always spoke first . . .*

XX

But it so happened that the little prince, having walked a long time through sand and rocks and snow, finally discovered a road. And all roads go to where there are people.

"Good morning," he said.

It was a blossoming rose garden.

"Good morning," said the roses.

The little prince gazed at them. All of them looked like his flower.

"Who are you?" he asked, astounded.

"We're roses," the roses said.

"Ah!" said the little prince.

And he felt very unhappy. His flower had told him she was the only one of her kind in the whole universe. And here were five thousand of them, all just alike, in just one garden!

She would be very annoyed, he said to himself, *if she saw this . . . She would cough terribly and pretend to be dying, to avoid being laughed at. And I'd have to pretend to be nursing her; otherwise, she'd really let herself die in order to humiliate me.*

And then he said to himself, *I thought I was rich because I had just one flower, and all I own is an ordinary rose. That and my three volcanoes, which*

What a peculiar planet! It's all dry and
sharp and hard.

come up to my knee, one of which may be permanently extinct. It doesn't make me much of a prince . . . And he lay down in the grass and wept.

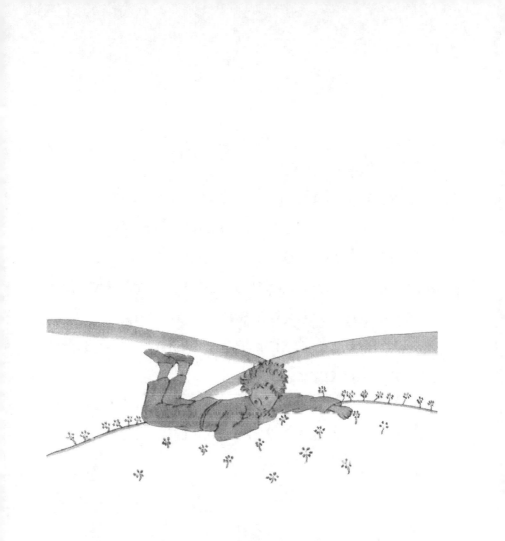

And he lay down in the grass and wept.

XXI

It was then that the fox appeared.

"Good morning," said the fox.

"Good morning," the little prince answered politely, though when he turned around he saw nothing.

"I'm here," the voice said, "under the apple tree."

"Who are you?" the little prince asked. "You're very pretty . . ."

"I'm a fox," the fox said.

"Come and play with me," the little prince proposed. "I'm feeling so sad."

"I can't play with you," the fox said. "I'm not tamed."

"Ah! Excuse me," said the little prince. But upon reflection he added, "What does *tamed* mean?"

"You're not from around here," the fox said. "What are you looking for?"

"I'm looking for people," said the little prince. "What docs *tamed* mean?"

"People," said the fox, "have guns and they hunt. It's quite trouble-some. And they also raise chickens. That's the only interesting thing about them. Are you looking for chickens?"

"No," said the little prince, "I'm

looking for friends. What does *tamed* mean?"

"It's something that's been too often neglected. It means, 'to create ties' . . ."

" 'To create ties'?"

"That's right," the fox said. "For me you're only a little boy just like a hundred thousand other little boys. And I have no need of you. And you have no need of me, either. For you I'm only a fox like a hundred thousand other foxes. But if you tame me, we'll need each other. You'll be the only boy in the world for

me. I'll be the only fox in the world for you . . ."

"I'm beginning to understand," the little prince said. "There's a flower . . . I think she's tamed me . . ."

"Possibly," the fox said. "On Earth, one sees all kinds of things."

"Oh, this isn't on Earth," the little prince said.

The fox seemed quite intrigued. "On another planet?"

"Yes."

"Are there hunters on that planet?"

"No."

"Now that's interesting. And chickens?"

"No."

"Nothing's perfect," sighed the fox. But he returned to his idea. "My life is monotonous. I hunt chickens; people hunt me. All chickens are just alike, and all men are just alike. So I'm rather bored. But if you tame me, my life will be filled with sunshine. I'll know the sound of footsteps that will be different from all the rest. Other footsteps send me back underground. Yours will call me out of my burrow like music. And then, look! You see the wheat fields over there? I don't eat bread. For me wheat is of no use whatever. Wheat fields say nothing to me. Which is sad. But you have hair the color of gold. So it will be wonderful, once you've tamed me! The wheat, which is golden, will remind me of you. And I'll love the sound of the wind in the wheat . . ."

The fox fell silent and stared at the little prince for a long while. "Please . . . tame me!" he said.

"I'd like to," the little prince replied, "but I haven't much time. I have friends to find and so many things to learn."

"The only things you learn are the things you tame," said the fox. "People haven't time to learn anything. They buy things ready-made in stores. But since there are no stores where you can buy friends, people no longer have friends. If you want a friend, tame me!"

"What do I have to do?" asked the little prince.

"You have to be very patient," the fox answered. "First you'll sit down a little ways away from me, over there, in the grass. I'll watch you out of the corner of my eye, and you won't say anything. Language is the source of misunderstandings. But day by day, you'll be able to sit a little closer . . ."

The next day the little prince returned.

"It would have been better to return at the same time," the fox said. "For instance, if you come at four in the afternoon, I'll begin to be happy by three. The closer it gets to four, the happier I'll feel. By four I'll be all excited and worried; I'll discover what it costs to be happy! But if you come at any old time, I'll never know when I should prepare my heart . . . There must be rites."

"What's a *rite?*" asked the little prince.

"That's another thing that's been too often neglected," said the fox. "It's the fact that one day is different from the other days, one hour from the other hours. My hunters, for example, have a rite. They dance with

120

"If you come at four in the afternoon, I'll begin to be happy by three."

the village girls on Thursdays. So Thursday's a wonderful day: I can take a stroll all the way to the vine-yards. If the hunters danced when-ever they chose, the days would all be just alike, and I'd have no holiday at all."

That was how the little prince tamed the fox. And when the time to leave was near:

"Ah!" the fox said. "I shall weep."

"It's your own fault," the little prince said. "I never wanted to do you any harm, but you insisted that I tame you . . ."

"Yes, of course," the fox said.

"But you're going to weep!" said the little prince.

"Yes, of course," the fox said.

"Then you get nothing out of it?"

"I get something," the fox said, "because of the color of the wheat." Then he added, "Go look at the roses again. You'll understand that yours is the only rose in all the world. Then come back to say good-bye, and I'll make you the gift of a secret."

The little prince went to look at the roses again.

"You're not at all like my rose. You're nothing at all yet," he told them. "No one has tamed you and you haven't tamed anyone. You're the way my fox was. He was just a fox like a hundred thousand others. But I've made him my friend, and now he's the only fox in all the world."

And the roses were humbled.

"You're lovely, but you're empty," he went on. "One couldn't die for

123

you. Of course, an ordinary passerby would think my rose looked just like you. But my rose, all on her own, is more important than all of you together, since she's the one I've watered. Since she's the one I put under glass. Since she's the one I sheltered behind a screen. Since she's the one for whom I killed the caterpillars (except the two or three for butterflies). Since she's the one I listened to when she complained, or when she boasted, or even sometimes when she said nothing at all. Since she's *my* rose."

And he went back to the fox.
"Good-bye," he said.
"Good-bye," said the fox. "Here is my secret. It's quite simple: One sees clearly only with the heart. Anything

essential is invisible to the eyes."

"Anything essential is invisible to the eyes," the little prince repeated, in order to remember.

"It's the time you spent on your rose that makes your rose so important."

"It's the time I spent on my rose . . . ," the little prince repeated, in order to remember.

"People have forgotten this truth," the fox said. "But you mustn't forget it. You become responsible forever for what you've tamed. You're responsible for your rose . . ."

"I'm responsible for my rose . . . ," the little prince repeated, in order to remember.

XXII

"Good morning," said the little prince.

"Good morning," said the railway switchman.

"What is it that you do here?" asked the little prince.

"I sort the travelers into bundles of a thousand," the switchman said. "I dispatch the trains that carry them, sometimes to the right, sometimes to the left."

And a brightly lit express train, roaring like thunder, shook the switchman's cabin.

"What a hurry they're in," said the little prince. "What are they looking for?"

"Not even the engineer on the locomotive knows," the switchman said.

And another brightly lit express train thundered by in the opposite direction.

"Are they coming back already?" asked the little prince.

"It's not the same ones," the switchman said. "It's an exchange."

"They weren't satisfied, where they were?" asked the little prince.

"No one is ever satisfied where he is," the switchman said.

And a third brightly lit express train thundered past.

"Are they chasing the first travelers?" asked the little prince.

"They're not chasing anything," the switchman said. "They're sleeping in there, or else they're yawning. Only the children are pressing their noses against the windowpanes."

"Only the children know what they're looking for," said the little prince. "They spend their time on a rag doll and it becomes very important, and if it's taken away from them, they cry . . ."

"They're lucky," the switchman said.

XXIII

"Good morning," said the little prince.

"Good morning," said the salesclerk. This was a salesclerk who sold pills invented to quench thirst. Swallow one a week and you no longer feel any need to drink.

"Why do you sell these pills?"

"They save so much time," the

salesclerk said. "Experts have calcu-
lated that you can save fifty-three
minutes a week."

"And what do you do with those
fifty-three minutes?"

"Whatever you like."

"If I had fifty-three minutes to
spend as I liked," the little prince said
to himself, "I'd walk very slowly toward a water fountain . . ."

XXIV

It was now the eighth day since my crash landing in the desert, and I'd listened to the story about the sales-clerk as I was drinking the last drop of my water supply.

"Ah," I said to the little prince, "your memories are very pleasant, but I haven't yet repaired my plane. I have nothing left to drink, and I, too, would be glad to walk very slowly to-ward a water fountain!"

"My friend the fox told me —"

"Little fellow, this has nothing to do with the fox!"

"Why?"

"Because we're going to die of thirst."

The little prince didn't follow my

reasoning, and answered me, "It's good to have had a friend, even if you're going to die. Myself, I'm very glad to have had a fox for a friend."

He doesn't realize the danger, I said to myself. *He's never hungry or thirsty. A little sunlight is enough for him . . .*

But the little prince looked at me and answered my thought. "I'm thirsty, too . . . Let's find a well . . ."

I made an exasperated gesture. It is absurd looking for a well, at random, in the vastness of the desert. But even so, we started walking.

When we had walked for several hours in silence, night fell and stars began to appear. I noticed them as in a dream, being somewhat feverish on account of my thirst. The little prince's words danced in my memory.

"So you're thirsty, too?" I asked.

But he didn't answer my question. He merely said to me, "Water can also be good for the heart . . ."

I didn't understand his answer, but I said nothing. . . . I knew by this time that it was no use questioning him.

He was tired. He sat down. I sat down next to him. And after a silence, he spoke again. "The stars are beautiful because of a flower you don't see . . ."

I answered, "Yes, of course," and without speaking another word I stared at the ridges of sand in the moonlight.

"The desert is beautiful," the little prince added.

And it was true. I've always loved the desert. You sit down on a sand dune. You see nothing. You hear nothing. And yet something shines, something sings in that silence. . . .

"What makes the desert beautiful," the little prince said, "is that it hides a well somewhere . . ."

I was surprised by suddenly understanding that mysterious radiance of the sands. When I was a little boy I lived in an old house, and there was a legend that a treasure was buried in it somewhere. Of course, no one was ever able to find the treasure, perhaps no one even searched. But it cast a spell over that whole house. My house hid a secret in the depths of its heart. . . .

"Yes," I said to the little prince, "whether it's a house or the stars or the desert, what makes them beautiful is invisible!"

"I'm glad," he said, "you agree with my fox."

As the little prince was falling asleep, I picked him up in my arms, and started walking again. I was moved. It was as if I was carrying a fragile treasure. It actually seemed to me there was nothing more fragile on Earth. By the light of the moon, I gazed at that pale forehead, those closed eyes, those locks of hair trembling in the wind, and I said to myself, *What I'm looking at is only a shell. What's most important is invisible . . .*

As his lips parted in a half smile, I said to myself, again, *What moves me so deeply about this sleeping little prince is his loyalty to a flower — the image of a rose shining within him like the flame within a lamp, even when he's asleep . . .* And I realized he was even more fragile than I had thought. Lamps must be protected: A gust of wind can blow them out. . . .

And walking on like that, I found the well at daybreak.

XXV

The little prince said, "People start out in express trains, but they no longer know what they're looking for. Then they get all excited and rush around in circles . . ." And he added, "It's not worth the trouble . . ."

The well we had come to was not at all like the wells of the Sahara. The wells of the Sahara are no more than holes dug in the sand. This one looked more like a village well. But there was no village here, and I

He laughed, grasped the rope, and set the
pulley working.

thought I was dreaming.

"It's strange," I said to the little prince, "everything is ready: the pulley, the bucket, and the rope . . ."

He laughed, grasped the rope, and set the pulley working. And the pulley groaned the way an old weather vane groans when the wind has been asleep a long time.

"Hear that?" said the little prince. "We've awakened this well and it's singing."

I didn't want him to tire himself out. "Let me do that," I said to him. "It's too heavy for you."

Slowly I hoisted the bucket to the edge of the well. I set it down with great care. The song of the pulley continued in my ears, and I saw the sun glisten on the still-trembling water.

"I'm thirsty for that water," said the little prince. "Let me drink some . . ."

And I understood what he'd been looking for!

I raised the bucket to his lips. He drank, eyes closed. It was as sweet as a feast. That water was more than merely a drink. It was born of our walk beneath the stars, of the song of the pulley, of the effort of my arms. It did the heart good, like a present. When I was a little boy, the Christmas-tree lights, the music of midnight mass, the tenderness of people's smiles made up, in the same way, the whole radiance of the Christmas present I received.

"People where you live," the little prince said, "grow five thousand roses in one garden . . . yet they don't find what they're looking for . . ."

"They don't find it," I answered.

"And yet what they're looking for could be found in a single rose, or a little water . . ."

"Of course," I answered.

And the little prince added, "But eyes are blind. You have to look with the heart."

I had drunk the water. I could breathe easy now. The sand, at daybreak, is honey colored. And that color was making me happy, too. Why then did I also feel so sad?

"You must keep your promise," said the little prince, sitting up again beside me.

"What promise?"

"You know . . . a muzzle for my sheep . . . I'm responsible for this flower!"

I took my drawings out of my pocket. The little prince glanced at them and laughed as he said, "Your baobabs look more like cabbages."

"Oh!" I had been so proud of the baobabs!

"Your fox . . . his ears . . . look more like horns . . . and they're too long!" And he laughed again.

"You're being unfair, my little prince," I said. "I never knew how to draw anything but boas from the inside and boas from the outside."

"Oh, that'll be all right," he said. "Children understand."

So then I drew a muzzle. And with a heavy heart I handed it to him. "You've made plans I don't know about . . ."

But he didn't answer. He said, "You know, my fall to Earth . . . To-

morrow will be the first anniversary
. . ." Then, after a silence, he con-
tinued. "I landed very near here . . ."
And he blushed.

And once again, without understanding why, I felt a strange grief.
However, a question occurred to me:
"Then it wasn't by accident that on
the morning I met you, eight days
ago, you were walking that way, all
alone, a thousand miles from any inhabited region? Were you returning
to the place where you fell to Earth?"

The little prince blushed again.

And I added, hesitantly, "Perhaps
on account . . . of the anniversary?"

The little prince blushed once
more. He never answered questions,
but when someone blushes, doesn't
that mean "yes"?

"Ah," I said to the little prince,

"I'm afraid . . ."

But he answered, "You must get to work now. You must get back to your engine. I'll wait here. Come back to-morrow night."

But I wasn't reassured. I remembered the fox. You risk tears if you let yourself be tamed.

XXVI

Beside the well, there was a ruin, an old stone wall. When I came back from my work the next evening, I caught sight of my little prince from a distance. He was sitting on top of the wall, legs dangling. And I heard him talking. "Don't you remember?" he was saying. "This isn't exactly the place!" Another voice must have answered him then, for he replied, "Oh yes, it's the right day, but this isn't the place . . ."

I continued walking toward the wall. I still could neither see nor hear anyone, yet the little prince answered again: "Of course. You'll see where my tracks begin on the sand. Just wait for me there. I'll be there tonight."

I was twenty yards from the wall and still saw no one.

Then the little prince said, after a silence, "Your poison is good? You're sure it won't make me suffer long?"

I stopped short, my heart pounding, but I still didn't understand.

"Now go away," the little prince said. "I want to get down from here!"

Then I looked down toward the foot of the wall, and gave a great start! There, coiled in front of the little

143

"Now go away . . . I want to get down from here!"

prince, was one of those yellow snakes that can kill you in thirty seconds. As I dug into my pocket for my revolver, I stepped back, but at the noise I made, the snake flowed over the sand like a trickling fountain, and without even hurrying, slipped away between the stones with a faint metallic sound.

I reached the wall just in time to catch my little prince in my arms, his face white as snow.

"What's going on here? You're talking to snakes now?"

I had loosened the yellow scarf he always wore. I had moistened his temples and made him drink some water. And now I didn't dare ask him anything more. He gazed at me with a serious expression and put his arms round my neck. I felt his heart beating like a dying bird's, when it's been shot. He said to me:

"I'm glad you found what was the matter with your engine. Now you'll be able to fly again . . ."

"How did you know?" I was just coming to tell him that I had been successful beyond all hope!

He didn't answer my question; all he said was "I'm leaving today, too." And then, sadly, "It's much further . . . It's much more difficult."

I realized that something extraordinary was happening. I was holding him in my arms like a little child, yet it seemed to me that he was dropping headlong into an abyss, and I could do nothing to hold him back.

His expression was very serious now, lost and remote. "I have your sheep. And I have the crate for it.

And the muzzle . . ." And he smiled sadly.

I waited a long time. I could feel that he was reviving a little. "Little fellow, you were frightened . . ." Of course he was frightened!

But he laughed a little. "I'll be much more frightened tonight . . ."

Once again I felt chilled by the sense of something irreparable. And I realized I couldn't bear the thought of never hearing that laugh again. For me it was like a spring of fresh water in the desert.

"Little fellow, I want to hear you laugh again . . ."

But he said to me, "Tonight, it'll be a year. My star will be just above the place where I fell last year . . ."

"Little fellow, it's a bad dream, isn't it? All this conversation with the snake and the meeting place and the star . . ."

But he didn't answer my question. All he said was "The important thing is what can't be seen . . ."

"Of course . . ."

"It's the same as for the flower. If you love a flower that lives on a star, then it's good, at night, to look up at the sky. All the stars are blossoming."

"Of course . . ."

"It's the same for the water. The water you gave me to drink was like music, on account of the pulley and the rope . . . You remember . . . It was good."

"Of course . . ."

"At night, you'll look up at the stars. It's too small, where I live, for me to show you where my star is. It's better that way. My star will be . . .

one of the stars, for you. So you'll like looking at all of them. They'll all be your friends. And besides, I have a present for you." He laughed again.

"Ah, little fellow, little fellow, I love hearing that laugh!"

"That'll be my present. Just that . . . It'll be the same as for the water."

"What do you mean?"

"People have stars, but they aren't the same. For travelers, the stars are guides. For other people, they're nothing but tiny lights. And for still others, for scholars, they're problems. For my businessman, they were gold. But all those stars are silent stars. You, though, you'll have stars like nobody else."

"What do you mean?"

"When you look up at the sky at night, since I'll be living on one of them, since I'll be laughing on one of them, for you it'll be as if all the stars are laughing. You'll have stars that can laugh!"

And he laughed again.

"And when you're consoled (everyone eventually is consoled), you'll be glad you've known me. You'll always be my friend. You'll feel like laughing with me. And you'll open your window sometimes just for the fun of it . . . And your friends will be amazed to see you laughing while you're looking up at the sky. Then you'll tell them, 'Yes, it's the stars; they always make me laugh!' And they'll think you're crazy. It'll be a nasty trick I played on you . . ."

And he laughed again.

"And it'll be as if I had given you, instead of stars, a lot of tiny bells that know how to laugh . . ."

And he laughed again. Then he grew serious once more. "Tonight . . . you know . . . don't come."

"I won't leave you."

"It'll look as if I'm suffering. It'll look a little as if I'm dying. It'll look that way. Don't come to see that; it's not worth the trouble."

"I won't leave you."

But he was anxious. "I'm telling you this . . . on account of the snake. He mustn't bite you. Snakes are nasty sometimes. They bite just for fun . . ."

"I won't leave you."

But something reassured him. "It's true they don't have enough poison for a second bite . . ."

That night I didn't see him leave. He got away without making a sound.

When I managed to catch up with him, he was walking fast, with determination. All he said was "Ah, you're here." And he took my hand. But he was still anxious. "You were wrong to come. You'll suffer. I'll look as if I'm dead, and that won't be true . . ."

I said nothing.

"You understand. It's too far. I can't take this body with me. It's too heavy."

I said nothing.

"But it'll be like an old abandoned shell. There's nothing sad about an old shell . . ."

I said nothing.

He was a little disheartened now. But he made one more effort.

"It'll be nice, you know. I'll be looking at the stars, too. All the stars will be wells with a rusty pulley. All

the stars will pour out water for me to drink . . ."

I said nothing.

"And it'll be fun! You'll have five-hundred million little bells; I'll have five-hundred million springs of fresh water . . ."

And he, too, said nothing, because he was weeping. . . .

★ ★ ★

"Here's the place. Let me go on alone."

And he sat down because he was frightened.

Then he said:

"You know . . . my flower . . . I'm responsible for her. And she's so weak! And so naive. She has four ri-

And he sat down because he was frightened.

diculous thorns to defend her against the world . . ."

I sat down, too, because I was unable to stand any longer.

He said, "There . . . That's all . . ."

He hesitated a little longer, then he stood up. He took a step. I couldn't move.

There was nothing but a yellow flash close to his ankle. He remained motionless for an instant. He didn't cry out. He fell gently, the way a tree falls. There wasn't even a sound, because of the sand.

XXVII

And now, of course, it's been six years already . . . I've never told this story before. The friends who saw me again were very glad to see me alive. I was sad, but I told them, "It's fatigue."

Now I'm somewhat consoled. That is . . . not entirely. But I know he did get back to his planet because at daybreak I didn't find his body. It wasn't such a heavy body. . . . And at night I love listening to the stars. It's like five-hundred million little bells. . . .

But something extraordinary has happened. When I drew that muzzle for the little prince, I forgot to put in the leather strap. He could never have fastened it on his sheep. And then I wonder, *What's happened there on his planet? Maybe the sheep has eaten the flower . . .*

Sometimes I tell myself, *Of course not! The little prince puts his flower under glass, and he keeps close watch over his sheep* . . . Then I'm happy. And all the stars laugh sweetly.

Sometimes I tell myself, *Anyone might be distracted once in a while, and that's all it takes! One night he forgot to put her under glass, or else the sheep got out without making any noise, during the night* . . . Then the bells are all changed into tears!

It's all a great mystery. For you, who love the little prince, too. As for me, nothing in the universe can be the same if somewhere, no one knows where, a sheep we never saw has or has not eaten a rose. . . .

Look up at the sky. Ask yourself, "Has the sheep eaten the flower or not?" And you'll see how everything changes. . . .

And no grown-up will ever understand how such a thing could be so
important!

He fell gently, the way a tree falls. There wasn't even a sound. . . .

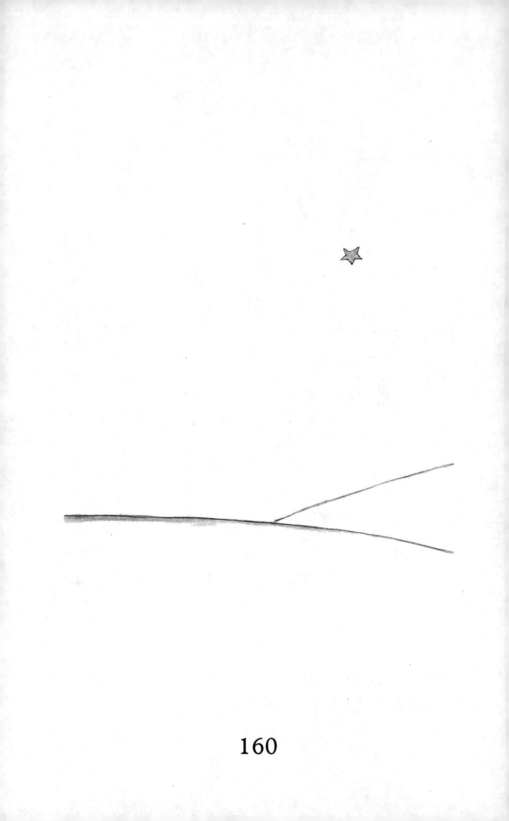

For me, this is the loveliest and the saddest landscape in the world. It's the same landscape as the one on the preceding page, but I've drawn it one more time in order to be sure you see it clearly. It's here that the little prince appeared on Earth, then disappeared.

Look at this landscape carefully to be sure of recognizing it, if you should travel to Africa someday, in the desert. And if you happen to pass by here, I beg you not to hurry past. Wait a little, just under the star! Then if a child comes to you, if he laughs, if he has golden hair, if he doesn't answer your questions, you'll know who he is. If this should happen, be kind!

Don't let me go on being so sad: Send word immediately that he's come back. . . .

Antoine de Saint-Exupéry

(June 29, 1900–July 31, 1944)

Antoine de Saint-Exupéry was born in Lyons on June 29, 1900. He flew for the first time at the age of twelve, at the Ambérieu airfield, and it was then that he became determined to be a pilot. He kept that ambition even after moving to a school in Switzerland and while spending summer vacations at the family's château at Saint-Maurice-de-Rémens, in eastern France. (The house at Saint-Maurice appears again and again in Saint-Exupéry's writing.) Later, in Paris, he failed the entrance exams for the French naval academy and, instead, enrolled at the prestigious art school l'Ecole des Beaux-Arts.

In 1921 Saint-Exupéry began serving in the military, and was stationed in Strasbourg. There he learned to be a pilot, and his career path was forever settled. After leaving the service, in 1923, Saint-Exupéry worked in several professions, but in 1926 he went back to flying and signed on as a pilot for Aéropostale, a private airline that flew mail from Toulouse, France, to Dakar, Senegal.

In 1927 Saint-Exupéry accepted the position of airfield chief for Cape Juby, in southern Morocco, and began writing his first book, a memoir called *Southern Mail*, which was published in 1929. He then moved briefly to Buenos Aires to oversee the establishment of an Argentinean mail service; when he returned to Paris in 1931, he published *Night Flight*, which won instant success and the prestigious Prix Femina.

Always daring, Saint-Exupéry tried in 1935 to break the speed record for flying from Paris to Saigon. Unfortunately, his plane crashed in the Libyan desert, and he and his copilot had to trudge through the sand for three days to find help. In 1938 he was seriously injured in a second plane crash, this time as he tried to fly between New York City and Tierra del Fuego, Argentina. The crash resulted in a long convalescence in New York. Saint-Exupéry's next novel, *Wind, Sand and Stars*, was published in 1939. A great success, the book won the Académie Française's Grand

Prix du Roman (Grand Prize for Novel Writing) and the National Book Award in the United States.

At the beginning of the Second World War, Saint-Exupéry flew reconnaissance missions for France, but he went to New York to ask the United States for help when the Germans occupied his country. He drew on his wartime experiences to write *Flight to Arras* and *Letter to a Hostage*, both published in 1942. His classic *The Little Prince* appeared in 1943.

Later in 1943 Saint-Exupéry rejoined his French air squadron in northern Africa. Despite being forbidden to fly (he was still suffering physically from his earlier plane crashes), Saint-Exupéry insisted on being given a mission. On July 31,

1944, he set out from Borgo, Corsica, to overfly occupied France. He never returned.

Translator Richard Howard is the author of eleven books of poetry, including *Untitled Subjects*, which won the Pulitzer Prize in 1970, and most recently, *Trappings*. He is the translator of more than 150 works from the French. In 1984 he received the American Book Award for his translation of Charles Baudelaire's *Les Fleurs du Mal*. Mr. Howard lives in New York City.

CPSIA information can be obtained
at www.ICGtesting.com
Printed in the USA
FFOW05n0101130515